SCHOOL BUS

DONALD CREWS

GREENWILLOW BOOKS/New York

For the
buses,
the riders,
and the
watchers

School Bus
Copyright © 1984
by Donald Crews
All rights reserved.
Manufactured in China
For information address
HarperCollins Children's
Books, a division of
HarperCollins Publishers,
195 Broadway,
New York, NY 10007.
www.harperchildrens.com
First Edition
17 18 SCP 20 19 18 17 16

Library of Congress
Cataloging in
Publication Data
Crews, Donald.
School bus.
"Greenwillow Books."

Summary: Follows the
progress of school buses
as they take children to
school and bring them
home again.

[1. School buses—Fiction.
2. Buses—Fiction]
I. Title.
PZ7.C8682Sc 1984
[E]   83-18681
ISBN 0-688-02807-1 (trade)
ISBN 0-688-02808-X (lib. bdg.)
ISBN 0-688-12267-1 (pbk.)

Yellow school buses

large and small.

Empty yellow buses cross the town.

STOP.

GO.

Going this way.

Going that way.

Here it comes.

See you later.

SCHOOL BUS

Full buses head for school.

Here we are.

Right on time.

Empty buses wait.

School's over.

Full buses cross the town.

Home again.

Home again.